A Visit From
RANDMA and GRANDPA

by CATHERINE KENWORTHY
illustrated by KATHY ALLERT

A GOLDEN BOOK • NEW YORK
Western Publishing Company, Inc., Racine, Wisconsin 53404

I J

Margaret felt happy and sad at the same time.

Her grandparents had come to visit, but her parents were going away on a vacation.

Margaret stood in the doorway with Grandma and Grandpa and waved good-bye.

Then Margaret became very quiet.
"What's the matter?" Grandpa asked.
"I miss Mommy and Daddy," said Margaret.
Grandma opened her pocketbook and took out her wallet. Inside was a picture of Margaret's mother and father.

"Here, Margaret, you may borrow this picture. Whenever you get lonely for your mom and dad, you can look at it," said Grandma.

Margaret put the picture on the table next to her bed.

"Now, we need a special little girl to help us unpack," said Grandpa. "She should be about this tall."

"She should have brown hair and green eyes," said Grandma.

"And her name," Grandpa added, "should be Margaret."

"That's me!" Margaret said.
"Then you are the special
little girl we are looking
for," said Grandpa.

Margaret showed
Grandma and Grandpa
their dresser and their
closet.

Grandma unpacked
her travel clock with the
red leather case.

Grandpa unpacked his
shiny silver harmonica.

"Now," said Grandma, "we need someone to show us around the neighborhood."

"I will!" said Margaret.

Margaret took Grandma and Grandpa to meet Mr. Hays at the grocery store…

...and Mrs. Wilson at the candy store.

Then Margaret showed Grandma and Grandpa where to buy ice cream cones.

That night Grandma and Grandpa and
Margaret went to the movies. They stayed out
way past Margaret's bedtime. That was fun.

The next day, Margaret's friends came to play. Grandma made pink lemonade and Grandpa played "Old MacDonald Had a Farm" on his harmonica.

Everyone clapped and sang.

Margaret was busy every day. She helped make raisin cookies. Grandma let Margaret lick the spoon.

Margaret helped Grandpa rake the leaves.
Grandpa didn't mind when she jumped
in the pile.

After a trip to the store, Margaret helped
to put the groceries away.

At the bottom of the bag there was
a coloring book just for her.

On the last day of the visit, Margaret showed Grandma and Grandpa the boat pond in the park. They watched the boats sail from one side of the pond to the other. They tried to guess which boat would be the fastest.

When Margaret's
parents came home,
Mommy said, "Grandm
and Grandpa tell us you
took good care of them
while we were gone."

That made Margaret
feel proud.

"Well, Margaret," Grandpa said, "It's time for us to go."

"Oh, no," said Margaret. "Now I'm sad again." But Grandma handed Margaret a package.

Inside the package was a picture of Grandma and Grandpa.

"Oh, thank you," Margaret said.

And that night she put the picture on the table next to her bed.